Barney the Bear Killer
Book 4

Cougar Holler

Barney the Bear Killer
Book 4

Cougar Holler

By

Pat L. Sargent

Illustrated by
Jane Lenoir

Ozark Publishing, Inc.
P.O. Box 228
Prairie Grove, AR 72753

Library of Congress cataloging-in-publication data

Sargent, Pat, 1936—
  Cougar Holler / by Pat L. Sargent ; illustrated by Jane
Lenoir.
      p. cm. -- (Barney the Bear Killer ; bk. 4)
Summary: When a cougar threatens the farm animals,
and then Farmer John and his family, Barney the black
and tan coonhound and the wild animal engage in a
ferocious battle.
  ISBN 1-56763-563-6 -- ISBN 1-56763-564-4 (pbk.)
  1. Dogs--Juvenile fiction. [1. Dogs--Fiction. 2. Puma-
-Fiction. 3.
Farm life--Fiction.] I. Lenoir, Jane, 1950- ill. II. Title.
  PZ10.3.S244 Co 2000
  [Fic]--dc21

                                              00-011196

Printed in the United States of America

Inspired by

the many, many nights I've gone out coon hunting with my dad and ole Barney. Since my mother and daddy were teachers, my daddy a principal, he didn't go coon hunting during the week. But when a Saturday night rolled around and the moon was full, we got our hunting clothes on, Daddy grabbed his rifle, and we climbed into the car and took off. As long as we made it home in time to get cleaned up and to church on Sunday morning, my mother didn't object.

Dedicated to

an elementary principal and teacher, my loving brother, O. Wayne Shull, who died with cancer April 28, 2000. Wayne loved the stories I write about Barney, and he especially loved the Animal Pride Series that Dave and I write together. Ole Barney lives on the farm with the animals, you know. I finished this story the day Wayne passed away. I was printing out a copy to give to him so he could read it before the book was published. He always told me if my stories were good or not, and I valued his opinion. But I know my brother can hear me, so I'll just read it to him. Here goes. Are you listening, Wayne? I hope so, 'cause you're gonna love this one!

Foreword

Down along the bayou, through the stretch known as cougar holler, the woods were overrun with wild animals. The farmers tolerated them as long as they stayed in the woods, but when they ran out of food and began killing farm animals, all the farmers grew angry! That's when the dogs were called in—hunting dogs that could track by scent and/or by sight. And, of course, the best one of all was Barney.

Contents

If you would like to have the authors of The Animal Pride Series visit your school, free of charge, call 1-800-321-5671 or 1-800-960-3876.

Barney the Bear Killer
Book 4

Cougar Holler

One

Reoccurring Nightmares!

April's heart stopped when she heard the noise. She glanced back over her right shoulder, then slowly turned and looked to her left. Sitting on a stump, not far from the trail, were two yellow eyes watching her.

April froze in her tracks. She couldn't scream, couldn't cry out! She couldn't run, couldn't move! Her feet were glued to the ground.

The yellow eyes widened as a loud rumbling growl bounded across the ground toward her. And then, those eyes left that old stump, hit the ground once, and landed smack on her face. The yellow eyes had teeth, and the teeth tore her face wide open! As hot red blood ran down her neck, she let out a blood-curdling scream, "Barney!"

There, was that Barney coming? Yes. Barney was running toward her. "Help! Help me, Barney! Help!" she screamed again. And that's when her mother shook her.

"April! April! Wake up, honey! You're screaming. And you're all wet with sweat!"

"No, get away! Don't hurt me! Leave me alone!" April screamed. "Barney! Where are you, Barney? Get it off me!"

April was gasping for breath as her eyes bounced off the ceiling and

around the room. Where was Lobo?
Look! There was her mama! Oh, no!
Would the wolf get her mama too?

April's mama gathered her in
her arms and held her close as she
whispered, "It's okay. Mama's here.
You're safe now, honey."

April sat up in bed, trembling, and Molly gathered her close. "Was it that same bad dream again, honey? I'm so sorry. I should not have let you go with your daddy that night. I knew better. But it's okay now, honey. That old timber wolf is dead. Do you hear me, April? He's dead. He can't hurt you anymore, honey. Ole Barney killed him, remember? That wolf will never hurt you again." With tears on her cheeks, Molly rocked back and forth as she cradled the sobbing girl in her arms.

"Mama, it hurt me again. It did. I was lost in the woods in the middle of the night and that mean ole wolf jumped on me. I'm scared to go to sleep at night. I don't like that wolf! Why does it keep hurting me, Mama? Make him leave me alone!"

April's face was wet. Her hair was wet. Her gown was wet, and she was shaking like a leaf in the wind.

Molly held her little girl tight. She had done this so many times in the past months. Ever since the night John had talked her into letting April go with him on a coon hunting trip. Well, there was one thing for sure. April would never again ask to go coon hunting with her daddy. Never. She had gone that one time and had almost died. Molly sighed. If only she could think of a magic trick, or if she could wave a wand and make the horrible reoccurring nightmare stop. She hoped April would now realize that she had been right when she had told her that coon hunting was not for little girls, that coon hunting was for men and boys! But, would she? Hopefully, she would.

Molly eased April's head onto the pillow and then pulled the covers up around her. She leaned down and kissed her on her wet cheek and said, "Go back to sleep. You'll be okay. It's almost daylight. I'll stay right here beside you until you fall asleep, and then I'll start breakfast."

April closed her red, swollen eyes and a deep sigh escaped her. When Molly heard even breathing, she eased off the bed and left the room, closing the door behind her.

April had drifted off in her safe bed, but only a short time later, she found herself deep in the dark woods, lost and scared! No! Not again!

Now, Barney knew that April was having trouble sleeping at night. He had realized that months ago. He didn't understand what was wrong, but he sensed that all was not right with his little friend, so he had been sleeping under her window at night. And each and every night, when she cried out in her sleep, he would stand on his back legs and look through the window, just to make sure she was all right. He was certain of one thing: that timber wolf was not in the room with her, even if she did cry out. That ole wolf was dead!

But why did she keep screaming out at night? Why did she lie there and fling her arms from side to side and cover her face with her hands? Why did she keep jumping up in bed, staring all around the room?

Now, when he heard her scream, even though he had just looked in her window and knew the timber wolf was not in the room with her, he put his paws on the window ledge and looked in.

That morning, while Molly was fixing breakfast, a thought came to her. It just sort of eased its way right into her head. She was putting flour on her rolling pin, getting ready to roll out the biscuit dough when the idea came a knockin'.

"That's it! That's what I'll do!" she said out loud.

"And just what is it you're gonna do, Molly girl?" Farmer John asked with a grin, as he walked around the table to fill his favorite coffee cup with steaming hot coffee.

"Top of the morning to you, John, dear. And how are you this fine morning?" Molly felt as though she would explode! Why, she could dance around the room and on the ceiling itself. Oh, if only this idea would work! It would be so grand!

"Well now, just what is it you're up to? You look just like the cat that swallowed the canary. Yes sireee, you do," was his only reply.

"I've decided to try something concerning April's nightmares."

"And what is that?" he asked.

"I've been reading a lot about bad dreams. Things like writing your problems down on paper so that you can see them and read them out loud, and that's supposed to help you to understand what's bothering you. The book on dreams says that you have to face-up to a problem before it can get better. And I believe that's true."

Farmer John's cup stopped on the way to his mouth. So, that's what she was up to. She had come up with the solution she'd been hoping for.

The trick that would hopefully stop April's horrible nightmares. Now Farmer John was excited too. "So! You've figured it out, have you, Molly girl? I'm real proud of you! Now! When are you going to try out this idea of yours?"

"As soon as we finish breakfast and the chores are done. I want the others out of the house, John."

Farmer John grinned, "I reckon I could handle that. Like a ride in the hay wagon, maybe. June Bug could hold one twin and Nicki the other."

"Oh, be careful with them, John. Those boys don't know how to hang on yet." Then, knowing she was talking about two tough little boys, Molly smiled.

After breakfast, Farmer John said, "You kids get ready. I'll be back to get you as soon as I finish my chores. Better wear your old clothes. We're going for a ride in the wagon."

Farmer John could still hear the yells as he and Barney headed down the lane to get the cows. Those kids could get excited over the least little thing!

As the kids left the table, Molly reached out and caught April's hand. "You stay home with me, honey. You and I have something special to do."

April's face showed relief. She had been afraid to go outside for seven months now. At least when she couldn't keep her daddy or mama or ole Barney in sight.

Molly now closed her eyes and prayed a silent prayer that her plan of combining two different techniques would work. It had to. It just had to. April's health depended on it.

After the others had left in the hay wagon, and the dishes had been cleared away, Molly placed a pencil and a Big Chief tablet on the table. She stepped back and called, "April. Will you please come to the kitchen, now? I think everything is ready."

Moments later, the little blonde-headed girl appeared. "Here I am, Mama. Everything's ready for what? What are we going to do?"

"You'll see," Molly answered. "First, go to the door and call Barney. Bring him in. He's still out there. I asked your daddy to leave him here."

April looked surprised. It had been some time since her mama had allowed Barney inside—Probably since the twins arrived.

"Hey, Barney! You want in?"

Before the words had cleared April's mouth, ole Barney sailed onto the back porch and into the kitchen. He stopped just inside the door.

Molly stood beside the table and patted the place where April always ate. "Right here, honey. I want you to sit right here."

April took her place at the table and, without a moment's hesitation, Barney plopped down beside her.

Well, this is it. Do or die time, Molly thought, as she took a deep breath. "Now, honey. We're going to try something that just may work. Do you remember all the books I've been reading about dreams?"

April nodded.

"I want you to try something. Now, listen carefully. Okay?"

Again, April nodded her head.

In a soothing but firm voice, Molly continued, "I want you to use that pencil and tablet and write down everything that happened the night you went coon hunting with your daddy. Write how you felt when you got separated from your dad and that ole wolf jumped on you and tore your face. And how it hurt! And how you felt when blood started running down your neck. Don't leave out a thing.

Even if you think it's not important, or let's say it's just too scary to think about. Just don't leave it out, honey. Don't leave anything out."

April's face had changed. There was a look of terror on it now—sheer terror. Wild eyes searched her mama's face. She must have heard wrong. Surely her mama had not said what she thought she had said. It wasn't possible, this awful thing her mama had asked her to do. No! Her mama wouldn't do her that way. She wouldn't! April's pretty blue eyes filled with tears, and they rolled down her face as she shook her head.

"I can't do it, Mama. I can't. Don't make me do it! Please don't!"

Now, at April's sudden outburst, Barney stood up. He put his head in her lap and leaned against her leg.

It's probably true that Barney did not understand everything Molly had said, but he had caught one word. He heard the word **wolf**! And now, he growled a low warning growl.

Barney's growl seemed to pull April together. She bowed her head, and her arms went around his neck. He reached up and licked her teary face, just like he had done that scary night when he had licked the blood off her face and neck. Poor thing.

April now took the kleenex her mama handed her. She dried her face and blew her nose, then picked up the pencil and slowly began writing. From time to time, one hand went to Barney's head that stayed on her leg. When she finished writing, she laid her pencil on the table.

Molly said, "Now, come in here. I've built a fire in the fireplace. See? I want you to stand right here, April, throw your shoulders back, hold your head high, and read your story to me. Read it out loud."

April groaned. She had always done what her mama said, and now, in her heart, she knew that her mama must have a good reason for what she had asked her to do. She stood on the indicated spot, drew a deep breath, and began to read.

Two

The Miracle of Writing

When April finished her story, Molly shook her head. "I'm sorry, honey, but you are leaving out the most important part! You must sit here and write down exactly what happened between you and that ole timber wolf. Describe everything! The pain—the fear—everything you remember about that terrible night!"

Once again, April picked up her pencil. She wasn't sure why her mama wanted her to relive this. She didn't want to think about the wolf jumping on her and tearing her face. She had tried so hard to forget that! Why was her mama asking her to write about it? Why?

April got up and went to her Mama. "I can't, Mama. I just can't. My stomach hurts. May I please go to my room?"

Molly hugged April. She said, "I know it's hard for you to understand why I want you to write about these things. But I really believe that writing it all down on paper will help rid you of that terrible nightmare you've had over and over for the last seven months! I know that when I either talk or write about something that's bothering me, it makes me feel better. So if you write about how the wolf hurt you, it might make you feel better. Will you just do this for me?"

April nodded. "I'll try, Mama." She sat down at the table and stared at the tablet. She was beginning to understand why her mama wanted her to do this. It was like the times she and her sisters fussed and fought over something. They had to talk about it until all understood, then they had to hug each other and say, "I'm sorry."

Sometimes, just knowing why you have to do something makes all the difference. She understood now, that talking about it and writing about it would help make it better, so she knew she could do it.

She tore up her story and began again. There were times when she sighed and times when she sobbed, and there were times when she got sick at her stomach.

But you know, as she neared the end of her task, that of putting her terrible ordeal on paper, her pencil actually picked up speed! And as she stood once more and read aloud, she really did start feeling much better. She looked at Barney. She hugged him, and again, he washed tears from her face.

And Molly cried too. She was completely overcome with emotion. She went over to the fireplace.

"Okay, April. Come over here. I want you to hold your story in your hands and rip it to shreds. Tear it into little bitty pieces. And when you've done that, take it over to the fireplace and throw it into the fire and watch it burn! Burn it, April! Get it out of your head! And out of your heart! Do it, April! Burn it!"

April ripped several pages from the tablet. She clutched them in her hands and made ready to tear them in two, in twenty, in hundreds of pieces. But, now that the time had come, she just stood there, looking at her mama. Then she looked down at ole Barney. Something was happening to her. She was starting to feel better!

April held her story against her chest and shook her head. "You know what? I'm not going to burn my story, Mama. I'm keeping it!"

Molly was a little surprised and yet delighted that her idea had worked! She hugged April, and Barney licked April's face. And everyone cried. Well, all but Barney. Dogs don't cry when they're happy. Dogs bark! And that's what he did. Barney the Bear Killer barked!

Farmer John carefully handed the twins down to Amber and Ashley, then unhitched the wagon and ran to the house. He couldn't wait to find out what had happened with Molly's plan to rid April of the nightmares.

He ran in and his eyes searched Molly's face. Her excited expression told him what he wanted to know. He reached up, grabbed his old straw hat and sailed it across the room.

Molly hugged him tighter than she ever had before! Why, she just about cut off his air. He whirled her around the living room. It was the best feeling in the whole wide world! After seven long, terrible months, April's awful nightmares would stop. She would not wake up screaming anymore. Not anymore.

April smiled at her daddy when

he sat down in his chair. He patted
the arm of the chair, and she sat down
on the arm, then leaned against his
shoulder.

Farmer John asked, "Have you forgiven me J. J., for taking you on that coon hunting trip?"

April looked into her daddy's eyes and smiled. "Oh, Daddy, it's all right. What happened to me was not your fault. You can't help it because that ole wolf was mean. I'm the one who fell behind. It's not your fault, Daddy. I'm fine, now. I'm not going to have any more bad dreams."

April was on one arm of her daddy's chair and Barney was on the other side of his chair. And, at that moment, anyone looking at Barney could see the smile on his face. Yep. Barney was wearing a great big grin.

Farmer John had a big heart. And he could feel it swelling. It was a good feeling. He was thankful for so much: for his wife, his three girls, his twin boys, and of course, for his faithful dog, Barney. April would not be here today, if not for Barney.

A couple of weeks later, Molly was fixing supper and Farmer John was in his chair, dozing, when April ran in the back door. She ran straight to her daddy's chair. Now, Molly saw her standing beside Farmer John, but she didn't really pay any mind to what she was doing. She went right on with her cooking. She was busy turning the fried potatoes, knee-deep in thought when something April was saying caught her attention.

"Don't say no, Daddy. Will you at least think about it? Please?"

Farmer John jumped and sat up. He must have dozed off. What was it J. J. had asked?

"I'd stay right with you, Daddy.

I promise," she added. "And if I fell down, I'd scream real loud so you'd stop and wait for me to catch up."

Farmer John could not believe his ears. J. J. was wanting to go coon hunting with him again? Man alive! He grinned as he looked at the happy face that was bouncing up and down in front of him. April's eyes were absolutely glowing with excitement!

"Please, Daddy! Say yes!"

Barney looked at April, then he looked at Farmer John. Hmmm.

Molly had supper almost ready and was wondering whose turn it was to set the table when she overheard the truly unbelievable conversation. To put it mildly, she was absolutely stunned! Horrified! Why, it was inconceivable that April would even think about going out coon hunting with her daddy after she had almost been killed by that crazy ole timber wolf on her first coon hunting trip! And after the poor little thing had endured seven long months of scary, horrible nightmares!

"I don't believe what I just heard!" Molly said, under her breath. "I simply don't believe it! I thought I heard April ask to go coon hunting!

And her nightmares have just ended! What is wrong with that child?"

Molly flew into the living room. She stopped in front of Farmer John's chair. With her hands on her hips, she stared at the three of them—her husband, Barney the Bear Killer, and her truly unbelievable daughter!

"John! You wipe that grin right off your face! You, too, young lady!" Molly added, as she turned to April. Then she reached out and touched her husband's head with the back of her hand and, with a worried frown, asked, "John, do you have a fever?"

Now, when Molly reached out and touched Farmer John's forehead, he laughed and grabbed her hand. "Ah, Molly. We were just spoofing. Weren't we, J. J.?" he asked, with a wink at April.

Later that night, when the kids were fast asleep, Molly crawled into bed. She lay there for a few minutes, then raised up on one elbow and looked down at her husband. He was sleeping like a baby. No! Surely not. He wouldn't! Would he? Why, no! Of course not. She smiled then and lay her head on her pillow. As her eyes closed, a deep sigh escaped her. Life was good on this farm. Her life was complete. She had John and five happy children. Especially now that April would, hopefully, stop having those horrible, scary nightmares.

It seemed like only minutes had passed since April had gone to bed when she rolled over and opened her eyes. Why, it was daylight outside! For the first time in months, she had slept through the night!

The very next night, a scream woke the family. They were not quite sure what it was. But now, sleeping under April's window, was the overseer of the farm. And in only a matter of seconds, ole Barney was on his feet, the hair on the back of his neck and shoulders, bristling.

Ole Barney stood there knowing that it could not have been Samone. Even though Samone was older now, there was no way she could have made that sound. It had been a much bigger cat-scream than Samone or her brothers or sisters, or even her mama could have made. As a matter of fact, Barney was sure he had heard that sound before. But why was it so close to the house? He didn't like it. Something was definitely wrong!

Now ole Barney the Bear Killer remembered. He had been down in cougar holler, trotting along the trail, minding his own business, when that awful scream, like a person in pain, rolled across his head and bounced off the trees. It was terrifying!

"Criminy!" Barney said, "That old cougar is too close for comfort!"

Barney stayed on guard for the remainder of the night. It was a good thing to do for the family and all the animals, but it sure played havoc with his sleep. And it's a well-known fact that coonhounds love to sleep.

Now, most people are not aware of all the hard work coonhounds do. But ole Barney earned his keep. Yes sireee, he did. He took care of the family, guarded the baby animals, and kept an eye on the milk herd. And of course, one of his main jobs was to keep that pesky Roy Raccoon, Bandit, Sammy, and Kitty Hawk away from the chickens and out of the eggs in the chicken house. Yep! Ole Barney would just have to grab a wink or two when he could today. There was no way around it.

Three

The Granddaddy Cougar

Down in cougar holler, the big granddaddy of them all was pacing back and forth on the high rim of the rock wall overlooking the river.

From the tip of his nose to his bottom where his tail was attached, the cougar measured six and one-half feet long. And then, if you hooked the three to four foot length of his tail to that, man, you'd have one big cougar! His muscles rippled as he let out a terrifying scream that sent quivers up and down spines.

Even ole Barney the Bear Killer
didn't run the holler during the night,
cause he knew full well that night-
time belonged to the *wild* animals.
He didn't consider Kitty Cougar or
Dike the Wolf or Brutus the Bear as
being wild. Why, for the most part,
they were his friends. Well, they
were his friends most of the time.
Now, ole Barney was nobody's fool.
And when Brutus or Dike or Kitty
was in a bad mood, he simply stayed
far away from that particular animal
on that particular day. And Barney
was smart enough to know that
everyone has a bad day, sometimes.
Things can't always go right.

"Barney! Where are you, boy?"

The call startled Barney. Even
though his eyes were closed, he was
anything but asleep. He was lying

there thinking about that ole cougar and the threats he had been sending across the air waves. Hopefully, he wasn't considering one of the little farm animals or someone on the farm as his next meal. Surely he could find something to eat without having to resort to the unthinkable!

Barney knew that ole cougar. He had come face to face with him one night when he had been out coon hunting. He was hot on the trail of a varmint and had picked up the scent of a wild animal. He knew the scent, but in the excitement of the race, he didn't slow down. Barney was not afraid of wild animals, but now, he did have a healthy respect for them—especially this cougar. That night, caught unaware, Barney had barely escaped with his life.

Barney the Bear Killer was way ahead of Farmer John and the others, and his long nose had been twitching uncontrollably for ten minutes before he rounded a curve in the trail and ran smack-dab into the waiting jaws of the cougar. When Barney saw the big cougar, it was too late to stop. The cougar was old, but he knew ole Barney was coming. And he was crouched low, behind some bushes. When the black and tan coonhound rounded the curve in the trail, that old granddaddy cougar lunged. He was on Barney like blackstrap molasses on bread. And even though Barney was not really expecting the attack, he fought back. Yes sireee, Bob! Barney and that old cougar went at it! Saliva dripped from their mouths as they tore into each other.

Again, Amber called, "Barney!"

Barney was busy, remembering. But when he heard Amber's second call, he stood up, stretched, and took off. He headed straight for the bus stop at a dead run, but the three girls were already coming down the road. He couldn't believe it! This was the first time he had missed their arrival.

Amber had come home from school with an important assignment. She was to do a two hundred word report on *cougars*. She had one week to do her research and get her report ready.

Barney sat outside the window and listened to Farmer John telling Amber that a cougar was also called mountain lion, puma, catamount, and in eastern states, panther. How could one animal have so many names???

Now, Barney could help Amber with her report, if only he could talk. He knew that old cougar. He had sat downwind from the big granddaddy cougar one evening, at dusky dark, and had watched him sharpen his claws and then wash his face with his front paws. Now, Barney knew the cougar had good eyes and ears, and he knew, from experience, that he had sharp claws and teeth that he used for grasping and tearing prey. But how could that cougar wash his face with his paws, without tearing his eyes out? Hmmm.

Also, ole Barney the Bear Killer remembered the big cat's paws that night when they had unexpectedly come face to face the night they had fought. The old cougar's paws were well padded and huge!

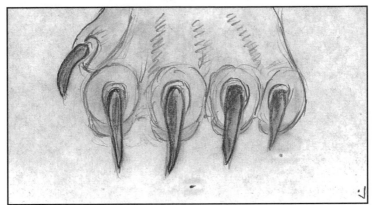

And a few days later, from his hiding place downwind from the old cougar, Barney had gotten a good look at the cougar's tongue. That old cat's tongue was covered with sharp, backward-slanted projections that he used to help clean the flesh from the bones of the animals he ate.

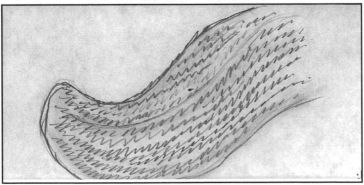

Late Thursday, the day before Amber's cougar report was due, she called ole Barney to the back porch. He was asked to sit at "attention" while she read her report out loud. Barney would be a good subject to practice on. He wouldn't talk back!

While sitting there, listening to Amber's report, Barney learned that not only did the cougar have huge paws, his forefeet had five toes and his hindfeet had only four. He didn't have the same number of toes on his back feet and his front feet. And he walked on his toes with the back part of his foot raised. His big ole claws were long and sharp and completely retractable. Retractable? Well now, that answered ole Barney's question. That cougar could draw his claws in and wash his face when he wanted to, and he wouldn't have to be afraid of scratching his eyes out or ripping his face. Then Amber's report told that a mama cougar has two to five cubs every two years. And like our house cats, the baby cubs are born with fur! They can't see, but they have fur!

Friday afternoon found Barney waiting at the bus stop for the girls. The driver honked and brought the bus to a stop. He waved at Barney. Barney would have waved back if he could, but since he couldn't wave, he just gave the driver a great big grin.

Amber was smiling and waving her report on cougars high in the air. She ran to Barney and gave him a big hug! She had gotten an **A**!

The bus driver always honked, and Barney thought he was honking just for him, but actually, the driver honked at all the farm houses to alert parents that the children were home. There were so many wild animals down along the bayou these days that parents were becoming more than a little alarmed. And of course, Molly and Farmer John were among those complaining.

The woods were overrun with wild animals these days. They were beginning to leave the woods at night and attack farm animals who were straying from the herd—baby calves, cows who were hidden away, giving birth, and even new-born baby pigs. It was awful to be awakened in the middle of the night by a screaming animal in pain. Barney slept under bedroom windows, on guard.

Finally, at the request of a dozen farm families, Farmer John called in the Game and Fish Department.

There was a big meeting, and a decision was soon made. The local game warden and the Fish and Game Department decided to relocate some of the animals. The farmers were told that this would be no easy task, and their help would be needed.

All area farmers with hounds, such as black and tan coonhounds, blood hounds, blue ticks, and red bones, were sought. Any dog who hunted by *scent* would be needed— even blue heelers and beagles.

One of the local farmers had an Afghan hound. He was told that his dog could be used to hunt by *sight*, but if the dog lost sight of the wild animals, he would not be able to track by scent. And that was okay.

The dogs were to track down, herd, or run the wild animals into a near-by holler, known along the bayou as cougar holler. The game wardens would be waiting in the holler with tranquilizer guns. Many of the animals would be tranquilized, then loaded into the backs of trucks with bars, and transported to another location—one with very few or no wild animals. All agreed that these wild animals were killing livestock because there was simply not enough food to go around. So, some would be tranquilized, and while asleep, would be transported to an area where there would be plenty to eat and no livestock to kill. They would wake up in new woods, with a safe place to roam. It would be a good thing for all! It would work!

When one of the officers with the Fish and Game Department stood to his feet, a hush fell over the crowd.

"Men, this project will be called **Operation Roundup**." Then, the officer sort of dropped a bomb. "There's one thing you should know. You farmers may lose a few dogs."

Four

Night of the Cougar

It was only a couple of weeks before the big hunt. The farmers and their families were getting anxious. Barney didn't really understand just what was about to happen, but now he knew something was going on. Something was up! He could feel it.

Sometimes, wild animals cried out, howled and growled during the nights, and no one got much sleep.

Barney was beginning to get a little grumpy. He still got up at the crack of dawn to help Farmer John with the milking. And, anytime there were outside chores to do, ole Barney was right there at Farmer John's side. And then, of course, he still made his early morning rounds. You know, to check out the maternity ward where the mama cows had new-born babies, the dry cows, the baby pigs, and the nearby woods. And he also checked the main hay barn and the big pasture behind it, but lately, Barney had sort of neglected that little chore. He knew that Marty Mule would kick up a fuss if a wild animal invaded his territory out behind the big hay barn. He knew that mule pretty well. And he knew that Marty Mule could defend not only himself but any of Farmer John's animals around him. No doubt about it. Marty could kick another animal's head off. That is, if he was of a mind to. Barney headed for Marty's pasture, and when Marty saw Barney coming, he threw up his head and trotted toward him.

Molly and Farmer John were on the porch, talking. "Let's tell them, John. Please! Let's tell them as soon as they get off the bus. Will you do this for me? I'm sick with worry. Let's tell them this afternoon, before it gets dark outside. They must be made to understand that going, or not going outside after sundown, is not an option. They **must** stay inside after sundown! Make it a rule!"

Farmer John searched Molly's face. Yes, she was definitely scared! Fear showed in her eyes, and her mouth was drawn. She was so tense! No doubt about it, he must follow through with this rule. He had never seen Molly so frightened.

"Okay, Molly, we'll tell them. Just as soon as they get off the bus. Tell you what, Molly girl," he added, "let's get Jake and Jack up from their nap. We'll get in the truck and go to the bus stop and wait for the girls. The boys have never seen that school bus up close. I reckon they'd get a real kick out of it! Would that make you feel better?" he asked.

Relief showed in Molly's pretty face as she nodded her head, grabbed the twins, and headed for the door.

Now, ole Barney was relieved when he saw Farmer John and Molly climbing into the truck with the boys. Lately, he'd been afraid for the girls to walk down that long road from the bus stop to the house. Why, anything could happen! Say, for instance, that cougar came out of the woods, made a beeline for the girls and grabbed one of them? Why, even if they saw it coming and took off running, it could pounce on one of them and drag her off before the others could make it to the house. Yep! Barney was glad that Molly and Farmer John were going to meet the bus. And he was right behind them. Together, they would make sure the girls got home safely. Yep! Those girls were his friends. He'd protect them against a cougar attack, with his life if need be.

Just as they reached the bus stop, the school bus rounded the big curve and stopped at the mail box. The bus driver held up his hand, and Farmer John and Molly waved, and the twins waved their hands, too! And of course, ole Barney smiled!

"Look at him. Look at Barney, Molly!" Farmer John said. "Did you see that big ole grin on his face when the bus driver threw up his hand and waved? Now, if that don't beat all! We're not the only ones who have seen Barney smile."

"I saw, John," Molly answered. "Barney is indeed a very special dog. He does have lots of friends. I don't think there's anyone in this entire county who doesn't like that dog of yours!"

Farmer John's pride in Barney was showing. His chest seemed to swell right in front of Molly's eyes. It stuck out a little further than usual. He said, "Aw, Molly. Ole Barney's not just *my* dog. Barney's *our* dog. Why, Barney the Bear Killer is part of our family!"

When Farmer John said things like that, Molly smiled inside. She loved to hear him brag about Barney.

After the three giggling girls climbed into the back of the truck, Farmer John noticed Barney and how he was acting. He seemed nervous.

"Molly, look at Barney. He seems a mite uneasy, don't you think? You reckon he knows about the roundup? You think he can sense it?"

"Well, I haven't thought much about it, John, but I suppose he can. Barney is a very exceptional dog. We both know that."

"Look at him, Molly. See how he's acting? Yep! That dog knows. Wouldn't it be a crying shame if ole Barney got hurt, or worse yet, if he got killed by one of the wild animals during the big roundup?"

Now, Farmer John grew quiet. To tell you the truth, he was wishing he had not even voiced the question. Something like that was best left unsaid. It had been an awful thought. He must not let himself think that way again. Barney would be fine.

Nothing would happen to his friend. It couldn't! Farmer John was quiet while he drove the rest of the way to the house.

When the pickup truck stopped, the girls climbed out of the back and Amber reached for Jack. She tried hard not to show it, but little Jack was her favorite.

Molly sat still. She glanced at Farmer John. He was sitting behind the wheel, staring off into space.

"Don't worry. Barney will be fine. Nothing will happen to him. Why, he's one of the smartest dogs I know. He can take care of himself. And besides, you'll be in the woods with him, won't you, John?"

Farmer John looked deep into Molly's eyes. She hadn't been in the woods in years. She had never ever watched Barney the Bear Killer run during a coon hunt. She had no idea how fast he was. Why, he could lose Farmer John in a matter of minutes. So just how in tarnation was he, the daddy of five kids, supposed to be able to run fast enough to stay up with that sleek and trim coonhound? And say, what if one of those vicious, wild animals had Barney backed into a corner? With no escape? No way! He couldn't watch him every minute! It would take some sort of superman to stay up with ole Barney!

Molly squeezed Farmer John's hand that still clutched the wheel. "He'll be okay, John. I can feel it. Barney will survive this. Come on. Let's go have that talk with the girls. No more going outside to play after sundown. Okay?"

"Okay, Molly!" Farmer John's shoulders visibly squared, right there in front of Molly's eyes. He got out, threw Jake up to his shoulders and, with the little boy hanging on to both ears, galloped for the back door.

When they rounded the corner of the house, Farmer John slowed to a lope, then trotted up the porch steps and suddenly threw on the brakes! He shouted,"Whoa there, you wild mustang! Who do you think you are, White Thunder?"

Now, the sudden stop was like a horse when it balks. And it almost threw Jake off his daddy's shoulders! Of course, Farmer John had a good hold on Jake's ankles.

The family had a long talk that afternoon and everyone agreed to stay inside after sundown.

Barney could feel the tension, and he wanted to be inside with the family, but now, he knew his place, and his place was outside, standing guard. He loved his little family and wanted to protect it.

And that's where Barney was when the yellow eyes peered from behind the trees and surveyed the barnyard that night. He was asleep under a bedroom window when his skin began crawling. He sat up and began scratching his back, thinking ants were all over him. Wide awake now, he suddenly sprang to his feet. Something was out there. His nose twitched, and his mouth quivered, as he crouched low and growled.

Barney figured that if it was the cougar out there, he could just go catch himself a rabbit! No, now wait. On second thought, he'd better leave the rabbits alone, because he might catch little Chrissy! Okay, so the cougar could just go eat a mouse! Oh, no! That wouldn't work either. He might eat Big Jake!

The smell of the cougar was in the air. Lucky for Barney, the wind was behind the cougar, and it didn't take Barney's nose long to tell where the cougar was. It was in the woods, near the pasture that ran alongside and behind the big hay barn.

Animals began moving about, making nervous sounds. The sheep started bleating, the cows started bawling, baby calves cried for their mamas, roosters began crowing, chickens cackled, and anyone knows that those chickens were not laying eggs in the middle of the night! And then, ole Marty Mule began braying! Barney tensed. His friend Marty was in the pasture behind the hay barn. Oh no! Not that. Not Marty Mule! Why, ole Marty had never, in his life, hurt anyone!

Barney knew he had to get to Marty's pasture in short order, so he took off at a dead run. That's about the time Farmer John hit the floor. He jumped into his jeans, grabbed his gun, and loaded it as he ran out the door.

The cougar crawled on his belly until he reached the back of the barn. And when he spotted Marty Mule, that ole six and a half foot-long cat streaked across the field toward him.

The cougar sprang when he was six feet from Marty. And man alive! That mule had never moved so fast! He whirled, kicked with both back feet, and hit that cougar in mid-air!

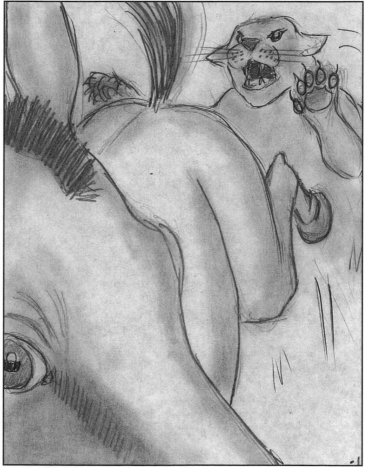

The cougar sailed high! When he hit the ground, ole Barney lunged. He landed right on top of the cougar.

Man! That was some bad fight! The cougar was giving it everything he had! But now, so was ole Barney. Barney was not about to let that big cat eat any of his friends on the farm! No sireee! Not if he had anything to say about it!

The cougar soon got enough of Barney, and when he pulled away and ran for the woods, Farmer John fired! The bullet only nicked the cat.

First, Farmer John examined ole Barney, and then he checked Marty. Marty Mule didn't have a cut on him, and Barney had only a few scratches, but some of them were pretty deep.

Farmer John said, as he headed for the barn, "Come on, Barney boy. Let's get you fixed up. Reckon I'd better clean those scratches so they won't get infected."

Ole Barney stayed close behind Farmer John. But he kept looking toward the trees, just to make sure that cougar was not coming back. That thing was mean! Why did he have to come so close to the farm? And why did he attack Marty Mule? Why, just the thought of that old granddaddy cougar attacking Marty made Barney mad. Hopping mad! Marty was his friend!

Farmer John got his disinfectant and his first aid kit and said, "Okay, Barney, sit down right here and let's clean your wounds a bit before we put this disinfectant on them."

Ole Barney knew he was lucky. That big cougar was twice his size! If Marty hadn't kicked him silly first, why, that old cougar might have killed Barney.

When Farmer John went in the
back door, Molly was there, waiting.
"John! Are you all right?" she asked.
I heard the gun, and I heard fighting!
Is Barney okay? What was out there,
John? Did you kill it?"

"It was that granddaddy cougar that hangs out down in cougar holler. He's big, Molly! That dadblamed thing is the biggest cougar I've ever in my whole born days seen! Why, he must be six and a half feet long if he's an inch! And that's not counting his tail! Man alive! What a beast! I'd sure hate to tangle with that thing on a dark night! Yes sireee, Molly! He's one big cougar!"

Molly just stood there, petrified! She actually felt her heart skip a beat. Oh, dear Lord. What if . . .

"Better take a deep breath, girl. Everything's gonna be okay. In a few days we'll have the roundup. And, hopefully, that cat will be taken away from this part of the country. An animal like that needs a big place to roam," Farmer John said.

Molly took several deep breaths and sat down. She had heard tales of cougars or mountain lions, as most people called them, attacking men, women, and children. The thoughts of her girls and her twin boys being mauled by a wild animal just scared her to death! Her mind was racing. And April! She had almost died that night she had gone out coon hunting with her daddy. What would she do if it happened again? How could she stand it if she lost one of her children to that cougar? Tears fell down her face as she tried to quieten her fears. She didn't want John or the kids to know how frightened she was. They needed her to be strong.

"Let's go back to bed, Molly. It's not even close to gettin' up time. Come on, we'd better get some sleep.

Tomorrow's a new day and we'd best be prepared for whatever it brings."

Molly looked at Farmer John. He took her hand and they walked down the hall, both wondering just what tomorrow would bring.

Finally, just before dawn, Molly fell asleep. When Farmer John eased out of bed, she was dead to the world.

Well, that morning Farmer John made his own coffee. And when he left the house to get the cows in for the morning milking, Barney was the only one moving about. That took some doin', cause ole Barney hadn't slept a wink all night—at least, not since the midnight visitor.

The two headed down the lane to get the cows in: one man, one dog. Friends who would give their lives for each other, if need be.

When they neared the maternity pasture, they saw that two of the cows had just calved. The babies were standing up, wobbling around, trying to nurse their mamas.

"Take a good look at those new babies, Barney. This may be the last time you'll see them alive."

Barney knew by the tone of his voice that Farmer John was serious. And though he wasn't sure, Barney suspected that it had something to do with that cougar . . or mountain lion. or puma . . whichever.

That morning while doing the milking, Farmer John noticed that the cows were real skiddish. They kept rolling their eyes and stomping their feet. Come to find out, that was just about the time one of the brand new baby calves disappeared!

The old cougar had waited his chance, then had crawled under the fence of the maternity pasture.

The mama cow had fought the cougar with every ounce of energy

she had, but he pounced on the calf
and broke its neck. Then, dragging it
with him, he made his way across the
pasture and into the woods.

And with the milking going on, ole Barney and Farmer John hadn't heard a sound coming from the maternity pasture.

Finally, ole Barney decided to leave the milk parlor and stand guard outside. He climbed to a knoll where he could see the back of the house and the barnyard where Marty was, where last night's attack took place.

All was quiet on the northern front, on the eastern front, and on the southern front. But now, something did not seem right to ole Barney as he looked off to the west. What was it? He couldn't tell. Wait! There it was! Something was in the underbrush! Bushes and branches were moving. Something was out there all right. Was it waiting for a chance to make a kill? Or had it already made the kill?

The back door suddenly opened, and like a streak of lightning, Barney took off at a dead run for the house! He sailed over the back fence as little Jake followed Ashley out the door.

Ashley looked up when Barney landed in the back yard. She said, "Hi, Barney. You jumped the fence! I saw you! I can't jump that high. We're gonna play in the yard. Wanna play with us?"

Normally, Barney would have been delighted to play with the kids. But not this time. He was worried. He completely ignored the question. He ran up the porch steps and began scratching on the door, wondering if Molly knew the kids were outside.

Now, when Molly didn't come to the door, Barney almost panicked. He barked once. Then twice.

Molly threw open the back door, and when she saw Ashley and Jake in the back yard, she sort of freaked out. She threw a hand over her mouth to stifle a scream, then ran down the steps and grabbed up the little boy.

With a stern look at Ashley, she asked, "Why are you outside, Ashley, and why did you bring the baby out, after the long talk we had last night?"

Young Ashley looked surprised. She bowed her head and said, "I'm sorry, Mama. But I didn't think I was doing anything wrong. I thought we could not go out after sundown. You didn't say that we couldn't go outside in the mornings. If you did, I didn't hear you."

Molly tried to smile. She held out her hand, and the little girl took it. "I guess I'm just a little nervous, honey. It is still morning, isn't it? I'll tell you what. I'll just sit here on the porch while you and Jake play. Will that be all right?"

"Oh, that would be fun, Mama! You wanna play? We'll let you!"

Molly said, "No thanks, honey. I guess I'm a bit tired this morning. I'll just sit here and watch."

Molly knew that she must stay calm for the kids' sake. It wouldn't be good to scare them. So she sat and watched the two play. Jake tried real hard to catch on to each new game, but Ashley moved fast through the part where she explained the rules, so he didn't learn some of the games. But he had fun trying.

Molly eyes were on the woods. She tried to appear interested in the games the kids were playing, but all she could think about was how truly devastated she would be if one of the wild animals or that big cougar came bounding across the open field and attacked one of her kids. Why, that cougar would kill anyone it attacked! It wouldn't matter the age. No one could survive an attack from that cat!

Molly looked at ole Barney. He was not interested in the kids' games. He was there to protect the family or the farm animals if need be.

Barney knew something was out there. From time to time he saw the bushes moving in the edge of the woods. The wind had shifted, so he had no way of knowing that it was the cougar, eating the newborn calf.

"You're a good dog, Barney. You're watching for that mean ole cougar, aren't you?" Molly asked.

Barney didn't move a muscle. Molly doubted that he even heard. He was on the back porch, alert. His eyes were sweeping the edge of the woods for any movement, and his ears were pointing forward to pick up any sound of approaching danger.

Five

Operation Roundup

The men felt it! The dogs felt it! Excitement was in the air!

Molly walked out the door with a camera. She loved taking pictures, and quite frankly, was very good at it. Everyone there would remember this day—the day they had been waiting for. The farmers and their families, especially those who lived down along the bayou, would, hopefully, breathe a lot easier after today.

Amber, April, and Ashley, who were usually happy, were quiet today.

They knew and understood what was happening. But of course, every man there knew that things don't always go as planned.

Molly's camera clicked several times before the men got organized. Finally, they had their guns and their dogs at their sides.

The big man in charge from the Fish and Game Department stepped to the front of the group. He stood, looking over the men and their dogs, and everyone grew quiet.

"I must say, this is a real fine looking bunch of dogs you men have here today. And I'm sure they'll do you proud."

At this, the men looked down at their dogs and beamed. And, if the truth ever came out, every man there thought his dog was the best!

"All right, men! You all know the plan. I hope your guns are loaded and you're carrying plenty of extra ammo."

The men raised their guns then some patted their pockets or the belt around their waist that held bullets.

"Now, all you fellows who are either game wardens or with that department, step forward."

At least two dozen men carrying guns and ammunition moved to the front.

"Okay. I see you men have your guns, but are they loaded with the right stuff? And are you sure you have enough tranquilizer with you?"

The men nodded. They had lots of bullets with them. Some bullets probably held enough tranquilizer to put a full-grown elephant to sleep.

The man in charge nodded his approval. "You men know what to do. You'll make your way to the area we've designated as cougar holler. Now, you need to make yourselves as near invisible as you possibly can. And don't waste your bullets, men. Better make your first shot count. You may not get a second chance. Remember, all these farmers' guns have real bullets that they will use for self-defense only. And we all know what that means. They will fire only if their life, their dog's life, or some-one else's life is threatened by one of these wild animals we're rounding up. Oh, and there's one more thing. There are wild animals on this farm that have never caused any problems. You need to remember the areas John has asked us to stay away from."

The men were ready! Each man there knew in his heart that his life, his dog's life, or even his neighbor's life could easily be cut short today. One never knows about these things. There are no guarantees.

"All right, men. Any questions? If there's anything at all on your mind, speak up!"

Every man there was silent as he thought about the day ahead of him and the dangers involved. No hands were raised. No questions asked.

"All right, then! We're all set! Good luck, men! Let's go!"

They headed out. They seemed very organized. The game rangers were out in front, going off in one direction. And when they reached the edge of the woods, the farmers moved out with their guns and dogs.

The dogs were straining hard, pulling at their leashes.

All the dogs felt the excitement. And, as incredible as it might sound, some, like Barney, knew exactly why they were there. No doubt about it! They knew!

Molly and the other women and their children who had shown up today stood silent, watching until the men were out of sight. Molly felt fear in her heart for John and Barney and, of course, for the others. It was a terrible thought but she stood there wondering what she would do if John were killed by a wild animal today. She shook her head. She must not let herself think that way. As she looked around at the faces there, she saw the very same expression on every face. That of fear, fear for their loved ones.

The women had brought along food that they had prepared at home.

Molly told the women to take all the covered dishes into the kitchen. The food that needed to be kept cool would be put in the refrigerator, and everything else was to be placed on a sideboard that sat against the wall.

Molly walked up the steps to the porch, and as she opened the door, she turned and looked at everyone. These women were her good friends. She had known some of them all of her life. She smiled at them and said, "There's no rush, so take your time. I'm afraid it will be a very long day. It has started out good. Let's hope it ends that way." They all nodded.

A few of the women just crossed their fingers. But now, Molly and some of her closest friends paused, closed their eyes, bowed their heads, and prayed a silent prayer.

Down in the woods, the dogs were flushing out animals left and right. The men were running fast, trying to keep up with the dogs.

As young as he was, there were times that day when Farmer John had to stop and take a breather. But he was not alone. The others did it too.

Farmer John heard a familiar bay. He stopped and listened. It was ole Barney coming back toward him! "What in tarnation is Barney doing? Has that dog lost his senses?"

The word **no** would answer the question. It wasn't his senses Barney had lost. It was one of the animals he had spotted. It was the granddaddy of them all—the big cougar!

Barney and the old cougar went right on past, neither of them looking his way. Farmer John took off his hat and wiped his brow and said, "Man! It might be better if Barney doesn't catch that dadblamed thing!"

Lots of animals, some wild and some not so wild, were rounded up that day. The really wild animals who were multiplying too fast were tranquilized and the others let go.

The day went pretty smooth for the men, but three of the dogs were torn up pretty bad in fights with wild animals, and two of the dogs were missing.

When Barney and the cougar sailed passed Farmer John that day, they must have kept right on going, because Barney was one of the dogs that was still missing. But all things considered, Operation Roundup was a success.

Farmer John stood staring in the direction Barney was going the last time he saw him. He shook his head. Poor Barney.

Six

Cougar Holler

The next day, Farmer John just kept pacing back and forth, worrying about Barney. If only he would show up. If he were hurt, he could be fixed up so that he would soon heal. But, on the other hand, if he was torn up bad, he just might die in the woods.

Molly was worried about John. He was not acting like himself today. Why, he hadn't even checked the dry cows since he had come home from the roundup. And it was time to start the evening milking! Now that was highly unusual. He was definitely not himself. It seemed to Molly that he didn't really care about anything else except that dog of his. It wasn't that Molly didn't care about Barney; it was just that certain things had to be done, regardless. Under normal conditions, she could help with the milking if needed and anything else, but with the twins so little right now, she felt she should be inside the house with them. Farmer John was the only one who could do it.

"John, if you've finished with the chores, I'll fix us a plate. The women divided up all the left-overs, and everyone took a little something home with them. There's some tasty food left in the kitchen, and we're getting a little hungry!" Molly said, as innocently as she could.

Molly was not a nagging wife, but there were things Farmer John needed to get finished before supper. It would be too dark after supper to do much.

Farmer John sat there, without responding to what Molly had said.

She was really starting to worry. She realized now that he was more than just a little depressed. When the girls asked her what was wrong with him, she whispered, "Your daddy is worrying himself to death about ole Barney."

April's face lit up. It glowed. She jumped up and ran over to her daddy's chair. She clasped her hands together and said, "I know what we can do! We can go look for Barney! You and me! Okay, Daddy? Please? Come on, let's go find Barney!"

Molly smiled at the change on Farmer John's face. She headed for the kitchen. "Now, don't you two be running off before supper. Hear? We're having something good!"

With some effort, Farmer John stood up and turned toward the door. When he reached for his work boots, Molly let out a big sigh. She just couldn't help it. She was so relieved. He was going out to feed and see to the animals and do the milking.

Farmer John finished his chores just as Molly got supper ready. After he took off his boots and washed his hands, Molly called all the kids and reminded them to wash their hands, and then she set the food on the table. She stood beside her chair, waiting for the comments she knew would be coming.

The girls helped the twins into their high chairs, then stood behind their chairs, waiting for their daddy.

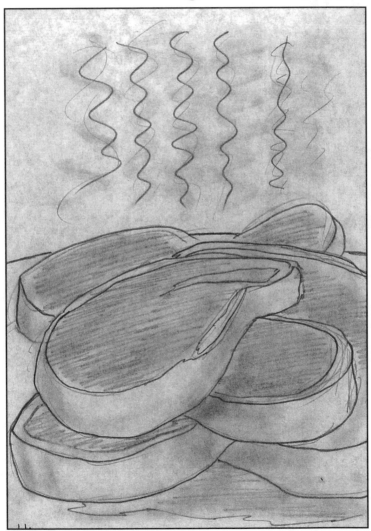

Farmer John and the three girls noticed the food that was sitting on the table at about the same time.

"Pork chops!" they yelled in unison. "We're not having leftovers; we're having pork chops!"

They loved the way Molly fixed pork chops. She chicken fried them. And gravy—chicken gravy that was out of this world! It was just a little brown, but it was not brown gravy. The slight tint of brown came from cooking the flour and browning it in the skillet before the milk was added. Now that made for real good flavor! And Farmer John loved it that way!

Molly glanced at Farmer John from time to time while they were eating. She knew he was trying to concentrate on the five kids and their conversations. But though he tried,

Farmer John was not acting like he normally did. He was usually light-hearted and fun. Molly and the kids loved his good nature. But tonight, Farmer John was not light-hearted. He was worried about Barney.

When they had finished eating, Farmer John thanked Molly for a fine supper, then looked at April as he got up from the table. He asked, "J.J., are you ready to go, or do you have homework?"

April could not understand how her mama and daddy always knew when she had homework. Maybe, under the circumstances, one little white lie wouldn't hurt. She put her hands in her lap, crossed her fingers and uttered, "I'm ready now, Daddy. I don't think I have any homework."

"Liar, liar! Pants on fire!"

April's face turned red! Fingers
were pointing straight at her!

April lowered her head and felt the tears welling up in her blue eyes. She wished with all her heart that she hadn't lied to her daddy. He was good to her. She knew that it was wrong to lie to him, even if she did have her fingers crossed. Even if it was just a little white lie. She loved her mama and her daddy very much. She should not have lied.

April stood up then. She looked at her daddy and said, "I'm sorry, Daddy. I don't know why I said that. I have some homework. Not much. But I do have a little."

"Apology accepted, J. J., but let's get one thing straight, little girl. I don't want anymore lies. You hear? If you ever tell me another lie, J. J., you'll never go coon hunting with me again! Is that clear?"

"Yes sir," April answered, as she wiped her eyes.

"I can forgive a lot of things," Farmer John continued, "but the one thing that's hard to forgive is a flat-out lie!" He grabbed his hat, socked it on his head, then reached for his gun. He grabbed a handful of shells and started out the back door. "Well, are you coming, J. J.? Or am I going to have to carry you?"

April hurried to the back door. When she reached for her school coat, Molly jumped up from the table and said, "Just a minute, honey. I'll get your other coat and your scarf. You grab a flashlight and your homework. You can sit in the truck with the doors locked and do your homework while your daddy combs the woods for Barney."

April grabbed her coat and her homework and took off out the door.

She reached the truck, just as her daddy climbed in and started it up.

"Sure you're ready, J. J.?" he asked as she climbed in.

"I'm ready, Daddy. Let's go."

Farmer John was beginning to wish he hadn't been so hard on her. She was a good girl. But now, she had to learn that truth was important, more important than fiction.

Farmer John drove down the lane and through the fields toward cougar holler. He got as close to the woods as he could in the truck, then stopped. He rolled up his window and got out. He leaned in, looked at April and said, "Now J. J., while I'm gone to look for Barney, you stay here in the truck. And don't get out! Whatever happens, don't get out of the truck! You hear me, J. J.?"

"Okay, Daddy. It won't take long to find Barney, will it, Daddy?"

Farmer John grinned. "I hope not, J. J.! I sure hope not!"

April watched her daddy until the night swallowed him up. "Bye, Daddy. I love you," she whispered. "I hope you find Barney." Then she turned on her flashlight and started on her homework.

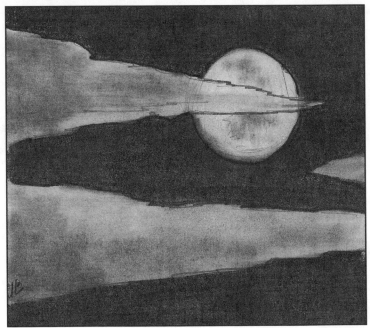

A cloud must have moved on, because that big ole moon suddenly got brighter. April noticed this and she hurried to finish her homework.

When she put her papers away, she leaned forward and peered out the windshield. She could see just a little ways down the trail her daddy had taken. Excitement was building. Her stomach was full of butterflies. She sat there, staring down the trail. She had an overactive imagination, and it was taking her even further.

Up ahead, the trail curved sharp to the right. April could see that it was narrow, a tight fit for two people to walk side by side. Her daddy had told her about the big cougar he had seen Barney chasing. That's why he had told her to wait in the truck while he went in search of Barney.

April's thoughts were racing. What if she met up with that cougar? What if he climbed into the cab with her? Would he be strong enough to break the windows? She checked both windows, just to make sure they were rolled up tight.

What if she came face to face with that thing her daddy had been calling "the devil"? She glanced over her shoulder. Her mama would skin her alive if she knew she were referring to something as a devil. Why, her mama wouldn't even call Satan the Bull by his name!

April's heart chilled when a blood-curdling scream split the air! Her eyes searched the dark woods ahead.

Then, again she heard a scream! Someone in the woods was in pain!

Wait! Did someone call her name? Was her daddy being mauled by the cougar, and was she supposed to save him? She rolled her window down a little but couldn't hear very well. So, in spite of her daddy's stern warning, she opened her door and got out.

"Daddy! I'm coming, Daddy! Is that you, Daddy? Is it? Is it you?" Then she screamed, "Barney! Help! Where are you, Barney? Help me! The cougar's killing daddy!"

April was a smart little girl, and at this moment, her mind was racing! She would need something to defend herself. She looked in the back of the truck, then under the seat. Nothing. Then she remembered—Her daddy always kept a lug wrench behind the seat. She pulled the lever that brought the back of the seat forward and then reached for the lug wrench. It was heavy!

Holding the lug wrench above her head, April ran down the trail, right down into cougar holler, crying, "I'm coming to help you, Daddy! I'm coming!"

Suddenly, she stopped moving. Something was pulling on her dress! Her body slammed to the ground, and a weight held her down. She kept struggling, trying to get up. She tried looking back, but whatever had hold of her began dragging her backward, and she couldn't see. It was dragging her back toward the truck!

When her captor stop dragging, April realized that she had dropped the lug wrench. She jumped up and ran for it. She had to have it back! She had to get it to her daddy somehow! To her utter amazement, there, running back down into the holler, was Barney. So that's who had been dragging her backward. He must have been trying to keep her safe, keep her away from the cougar!

"Wait, Barney! Come back!

Take this to Daddy! He can kill that ole cougar with it!"

Barney the Bear Killer was in a big hurry. He was trying to get back to help Farmer John. But now, when he heard April pleading, he stopped and looked back.

Barney didn't really understand just exactly what April was saying, but he knew she was trying to help. So he ran back, and when he reached her, she stuck the big lug wrench out. "Take it, Barney! Take it to Daddy! It could help save his life! Please! Open your mouth! Here! Take it!"

And now Barney the Bear Killer understood. And even though he was in a hurry, he knew April was trying to help too. So he took the heavy lug wrench in his mouth and ran back down into the holler.

April climbed into the truck cab and sat there, terrified! She was not about to get out again. Not now that ole Barney was helping her daddy. Barney was stronger than she was, and he would know better what to do. He was used to dealing with animals.

April shivered. If only she had some way of knowing just what was going on down there in the holler. She wondered if she could roll her window down a little so she could hear something. Should she risk it? Would a wild animal climb through it if she did? Or if that cougar killed her daddy and Barney, would it then come after her? She had no way of knowing for sure.

She sat there, trying to decide what to do. Then she heard yelling. It was coming from the holler.

"Barney! Can't reach my gun!
. . .Can't reach! . . . Get him off! . . ."

April knew her daddy was in trouble. She also knew that she was too little to kill that big old cougar. She took a deep breath, threw open her door and jumped out of the truck! She headed down into cougar holler, crying, "Barney! Help him, Barney! Please save my daddy!"

When April reached her daddy, his face and arms were covered with blood. The cougar had a hold on her daddy's arm. On the cougar, with teeth sunk into his neck, was Barney!

Farmer John's face was drawn with pain. And when he saw April, he screamed, "No, J. J.! I don't want you anywhere near this place! Run! Run to the truck! He'll get you, J.J.! He'll get you!"

Barney sank his long sharp teeth even deeper, and the cougar let go of Farmer John. It thrashed this way, then that, trying to throw Barney off.

Where was her daddy's gun? He had brought his gun! Her eyes searched the ground all around. And just when she was about to give up, she saw part of the gun sticking out from under a bush. She ran to it and reached down. She grabbed it and whirled around.

Farmer John's eyes looked bad. They were blurred with the blood that was trickling down into them. Now, they turned even redder with rage. When he saw J. J. with the gun, he wanted to scream, "Shoot!" but he knew that she had never shot a gun. He also knew that if she hit the cougar and only wounded it, it would be even meaner! It would be mad, and it would be hurting, and then it would kill them all!

Farmer John yelled, "Throw me the gun, J.J.! Hurry! Throw it!"

April drew back to throw the gun, but it was too heavy. She knew that it would not reach her daddy.

So, tossing caution to the wind, she ran toward her daddy, trying to miss the swirls and swipes of the cougar's claws! But she passed too close to the cougar, and one of its paws caught the back of her head. The hard fast blow knocked April forward, but the old cougar's sharp claws got all tangled up in her hair. April screamed and then the cougar screamed! The cougar jerked his paw back, hard! April fell backward, and out came some of her hair!

With that one paw, the cougar stuffed April's hair into his mouth. And with his other paw, he caught Barney's collar and yanked Barney off his back!

Farmer John's clawed-up hands reached out, and April shoved the gun into them. "Shoot, Daddy!" she screamed. "It's gonna kill Barney! And then it'll kill us!"

Barney picked himself up off the ground and circled the cougar. The cougar was mad, but so was ole Barney! He let out his "gotcha" howl that would make any other animal turn tail and run. But not this cougar. This holler was the cougar's home. This was where he had been born and raised. He was not about to leave it. After all, that's why everyone called this holler *cougar holler*!

Now, ole Barney the Bear Killer was not really afraid of the cougar, but he knew that it could easily kill him. Why, it was over twice his size! He knew that if he made one mistake, he'd be dead—so would his friends. Barney didn't think he was special or anything. But now, he did try to take care of the family and all the animals that lived on this farm. There was no doubt about it. Anyone who knew Barney could tell you that, at all times, he did his best.

Just as Barney was making his final circle around the cougar, things changed, right in front of his eyes. The old cougar whirled and headed for April. The scared little girl had run some twenty feet past her daddy, wanting to make it to the truck and safety. Her heart stopped when she saw the huge cat coming toward her. She tried to scream but nothing came out.

Farmer John threw up his gun, trying to get the thing in his sights.

And now, Barney made a desperate attempt to head off the old cougar, who seemed determined to eat April!

As the cougar streaked toward April, she screamed, "Barney! Help! It's gonna eat me! Shoot it, Daddy! Shoot it!"

Barney heard the frantic plea in April's voice. And once again, he was ready to save her. He knew that Farmer John would not shoot his gun because he was afraid he'd hit April. Barney would gladly give his life for April. He would, if he had to.

"No! Leave me alone! Barney! Help me, Barney!"

The big cougar sprang, and just as it landed on April, Barney lunged. Barney hit that old cougar in the side! The blow knocked the cat off April, but his dew claw caught her left arm and tore deep into the flesh. Those sharp claws went clear to the bone!

April screamed, "Barney!"

That did it! Barney was mad! That old granddaddy cougar had hurt April and Farmer John one time too many! And now he was gonna get it!

Barney barred his teeth, a deep growl came from his chest, and he lunged for the cougar's throat!

The two fought long and fierce. First, Barney was winning; then the old cougar seemed to be winning. Farmer John kept his gun on the two of them, ready, just in case.

Suddenly, the old cougar pulled away, and Barney crouched low. Instinct told the coonhound that it was time—time to go in for the kill. Then, a strange thing happened. Instead of lunging for the cougar, he froze in that crouched-low position! The sounds that came from his throat were awesome! But the cougar stood his ground. He glared at Barney, and Barney the Bear Killer glared back!

April's arm was spurting blood! She wanted to cry out, but she didn't. What exactly were Barney and the cougar doing?

Farmer John whispered, "Don't move, J. J.. Hold still!"

"But what's happening, Daddy? Why aren't they fighting? Look! They're just standing there!"

"It's a stand-off. Barney doesn't want to have to kill the old cougar. He's got too much respect for him. And, of course, there's always the chance that if he presses for a finish, the cougar may kill him. They're both pretty strong you know. And that old granddaddy cougar is big! He's much bigger than Barney!"

April was really worried now. She asked, "Daddy, is Barney going to let the cougar kill us, just because he respects him? Is he just going to stand there and let him kill us?"

Farmer John shook his head. "If that old cougar tries to kill us, J. J., there's no doubt about what Barney will do. Barney will have to kill him. Or, he'll try."

"And what if Barney tries to kill the cougar and can't? Then what, Daddy? Then what?"

"If he tries and fails, the cougar will kill Barney, and then he'll try to kill us, I reckon."

The expression on April's face changed. She now understood. Ole Barney's growl had turned into something she had not heard before. Farmer John had only heard it one other time. Barney was dead serious. Barney, known as *the bear killer*, meant business.

Farmer John threw up his gun and got the old granddaddy cougar in his sights. If the two fought again, and Barney lost, he must be ready. He would shoot that old cougar dead, if Barney lost the fight.

Barney the Bear Killer took a step toward the cougar. Surprised, the cougar took several steps back.

While Farmer John and April looked on, the same thing happened again and again. April whispered, "Look, Daddy. Look at them!"

The cougar whirled, streaked to the top of the rock wall, and flattened himself against a boulder. He lay there, hugging the boulder tight. Looking down, his shadowy figure was barely visible in the moonlight. His yellow eyes blinked and glowed, blinked and glowed.

Barney's eyes were on the cat. He was braced for what was coming. His long sharp teeth were bared, and saliva dripped from his mouth.

With his muscles quivering, the old granddaddy cougar glared down. He was crouched, ready to spring. Suddenly, he gave a threatening cry, then turned and, with his body close to the ground, slowly skulked away.

As the cougar disappeared into the night, Barney stood, like a statue.

"Tarnation!" Farmer John said in a whisper. "Did you see that, J. J.? Barney out-bluffed that ole cougar!"

April had seen it all right, but she didn't say a word. She just stood there, afraid to move a muscle.

Farmer John took her hand and said, "Come on, J. J.. Let's you and me wait in the truck for ole Barney. I don't doubt that he'll wait a while, just to make sure that cougar keeps right on going. You never can tell; he may double back.

While Farmer John and April were making their way to the truck, Barney decided to follow the big cat. So he trailed him to the river.

The cougar sensed that Barney was following him. When he reached the river, he turned and snarled at ole Barney. It was a real nasty snarl!

Finally, Barney the Bear Killer came trotting up out of the holler toward Farmer John and April. And anyone looking at Barney could tell he was hurt. He was limping a little. His right hip had a small gash on it. It wasn't bad, but it would be sore for some time to come. Barney was the bravest dog around. No doubt.

April let out a sob, relieved to see Barney. She was glad that cougar hadn't killed him.

"Well, Barney, you did it, boy," Farmer John said. "You got rid of that old cougar without having to kill him. I like that, Barney. I like that."

Barney licked April's face when she bent down to hug him. And then a big ole grin spread across his face. Farmer John really loved that look. It was special.

"Yes sireee, J.J., you're hugging one brave coonhound. Man alive! Barney sure sent that big cat packing! I wouldn't be surprised if that cougar leaves this farm for good."

"Where will he go, Daddy?" J.J. asked with her eyes on the holler. "Are you sure he won't stay around here and hurt us again?"

"Aw, I reckon he'll go off some place where he has room to roam and plenty of food to eat. Yes sireee, J. J., I think maybe we've seen the last of that cougar. I really do. He knows now that ole Barney won't tolerate any more of his nonsense."

"Ole Barney's special, isn't he, Daddy?" April asked.

Farmer John took off his hat and wiped his forehead on his sleeve. "This black and tan coonhound of ours is special, J. J.. Real special! He sure made that old granddaddy cougar turn-tail and run! Yes sireee, I'm proud of this dog! He's the best! He's our Barney the Bear Killer!"